ECFE

FROGTOWN FAMILY RESOURCE CENTER
377 UNIVERSITY AVENUE WEST
ST. PAUL, MINNESOTA 55103-2018

P9-BZH-763

the Salamander Room

by ANNE MAZER
illustrated by STEVE JOHNSON & LOU FANCHER

Dragonfly Books · Alfred A. Knopf · New York

DRAGONFLY BOOKS™
PUBLISHED BY ALFRED A. KNOPF, INC.

Library of Congress Catalog Card Number: 90-33301
ISBN: 0-679-86187-4
First Dragonfly Books edition: March 1994
Book design by Lou Fancher

Printed in the U.S.A.
15 14 13 12 11 10

For Mollie

A. M.

For Joel, Erin, Dale, and Tessa,
and a special thanks to Dave R.

S. J. & L. F.

Brian found a salamander in the woods. It was a little orange salamander that crawled through the dried leaves of the forest floor.

The salamander was warm and cozy in the boy's hand. "Come live with me," Brian said.

He took the salamander home.

"Where will he sleep?" his mother asked.

"I will make him a salamander bed to sleep in. I will cover him with leaves that are fresh and green, and bring moss that looks like little stars to be a pillow for his head. I will bring crickets to sing him to sleep and bullfrogs to tell him good-night stories."

"And when he wakes up, where will he play?"

"I will carpet my room with shiny wet leaves
and water them so he can slide around and play.

I will bring tree stumps into
    my room so he can climb up the bark
        and sun himself on top. And I will bring
            boulders that he can creep over."

"He will miss his friends in the forest."

"I will bring salamander friends to play with him."

"They will be hungry. How will you feed them?"

"I will bring insects to live in my room. And every day I will catch some and feed the salamanders. And I will make little pools of water on top of the boulders so they can drink whenever they are thirsty."

"The insects will multiply, and soon there will be bugs and insects everywhere."

"I will find birds to eat the extra bugs and insects. And the bullfrogs will eat them too."

"Where will the birds and bullfrogs live?"

"I will bring trees for the birds to roost in,
and make ponds for the frogs."

"Birds need to fly."

"We can lift off the ceiling. They will sail out in the sky, but they will come back to my room when it is time for dinner, because they will know that the biggest, juiciest insects are there."

"But the trees—how will they grow?"

"The rain will come through the open roof,
and the sun, too. And vines will
creep up the walls of my room,
and ferns will grow under my bed.
There will be big white mushrooms
and moss like little stars growing around
the tree stumps that the salamanders climb on."

"And you—
where will you sleep?"

"I will sleep on a bed under
the stars, with the moon
shining through the green
leaves of the trees; owls will
hoot and crickets will sing;
and next to me, on the
boulder with its head resting
on soft moss, the salamander
will sleep."